THE OBSERVABLE
CHARACTERISTICS
OF ORGANISMS

THE OBSERVABLE CHARACTERISTICS OF ORGANISMS

STORIES

RYAN MacDONALD

TUSCALOOSA

FC2 is an imprint of The University of Alabama Press

Book Design: Illinois State University's English Department's
    Publications Unit; Codirectors: Steve Halle and Jane L. Carman;
    Assistant Director: Danielle Duvick; Production Assistant: Taylor
    Kremer
Cover Design: Lou Robinson
Typeface: Garamond
⊗
The paper on which this book is printed meets the minimum requirements
of American National Standard for Information Sciences—Permanence
of Paper for Printed Library Materials, ANSI Z39.48–1984

Library of Congress Cataloging-in-Publication Data
MacDonald, Ryan, 1977-
[Short stories. Selections]
The observable characteristics of organisms : stories / Ryan
MacDonald.
    pages cm
ISBN 978-1-57366-182-9 (pbk. : alk. paper) -- ISBN 978-1-57366-849-1
(ebook)
I. Title.
PS3613.A27143O38 2014
813'.6--dc23
                                        2014005589

FOR MY FAMILY

CONTENTS

THE OBSERVABLE CHARACTERISTICS OF ORGANISMS

THE OBSERVABLE
CHARACTERISTICS
OF ORGANISMS

In the zoo we accomplish many things. The animals are always fed and locked in their cages. Habitats are well hosed down and visitors have a decent view, even though the animals sit completely still most of the time.

My daughter is four and has a low tolerance for such things.

"The animals look so sad," she says.

"They are not sad," I assure her. "They are maybe a little homesick, they are maybe a little lonely, but they are not sad."

Yesterday I went into the penguin habitat. It smelled like chlorine and sweaty feet so I opened the door a crack to let the place breathe a bit. A penguin squeezed through the crack and ran into the pedestrian path. It was too slippery to catch. I tried to stop it from entering the polar bear cage by throwing a large rock at it. But I missed and in it went.

"To be swallowed whole!" I said triumphantly to the gasping crowd, an arm raised for emphasis.

My daughter is in the employee lounge right now dissecting owl pellets. Plucking tiny mouse skulls from them. She wants to be a zoologist.

"I like to look at things from different angles, Daddy," she says to me.

I am not for or against this idea. I do however wish she would find an interest in botany or figure skating, something less repulsive, something not as smelly. My daughter walks with a disgusting limp. This is why she will always be single, I think.

My daughter, the limping zoologist. I will love her anyway.

Today we had ice cream at the concession stand near the entrance of the zoo. I watched my daughter eat the ice cream, chocolate all over her nose and cheeks. Even a little smudge on her forehead. 'Disgusting,' I thought, and wiped her down with a wetnap.

I took her into the greenhouse to show her the plantlife. We walked carefully down the aisles, holding our hands out to brush the tops of the greenery. My daughter sang a song as she walked, something about the observable characteristics of organisms with favorable phenotypes. Afterwards we witnessed the birth of a rhinoceros. It was magical, to be sure, and difficult to watch.

When rhinos have babies they tremble, they tremble the way all mothers tremble when having babies I bet.

When it was over, the rhino circled her calf, sniffing at it with magnificent nostrils. She lifted it to its feet with her horn. I wanted to be a mother. I've always wanted to be a mother, if only to tremble, to feel the warmth of the creature leaving me.

"It will never happen!" I said triumphantly to the rhinos in their hay-smelling habitat.

THE STORM

The storm is coming and I am trapped in the house with Richard Gere. It could be worse I suppose, he is *very* good looking.

We have been watching the local news to see what's happening outside. There is a hurricane outside; the scientists have named the hurricane Norman. Hurricane Norman is a level three hurricane, they say.

Richard and I have taped up the windows. We have secured all the china in the china cabinets. Richard is *very* helpful.

I am in the kitchen right now fixing us cocktails. May as well have some cocktails, I said to him.

You don't have to be a celebrity to have an alcohol problem, he said, smiling at me the way he does.

I gave him the finger and went to the kitchen to fix them.

Richard is *very* judgmental, always squinting at me and judging me. Sometimes, at night, I go to the window and look out at the mountains, and dream of another life. I look out at the mountains and dream of another place with another celebrity, one who is not so judgmental maybe, maybe not so knowledgeable.

Earlier we were watching the local news and Richard says to me out of nowhere, did you know, he says, did you know Pyrrhus of Epirus, a fearless warrior who fought the battle of Argos atop an elephant, was killed when an old lady threw a roofing tile at his head?

No I did not know that Richard.

The wind is picking up outside, I can hear hail tinking off the roofing tiles. Richard is leaning in the kitchen doorway, smiling and watching me with those dark eyes of his as I put ice in the cocktails. The ice cracks in the glasses.

I look up at him and he shows me his teeth in an expression I find excruciating.

CANTO

The moment my mother released me, they say, I took stock of the situation. I scrutinized the doctor's decisions. Dr. Havershamp held me in one hand and scooped mucus from my mouth with a cold latex finger. I did not cry but squinted deep into his eyes looking for secrets. One thing I already knew about this world, was that everyone had secrets.

When the doctor told my parents they could take me home, I repeated the word *home* several times, noting the pleasure of the long vowel.

I had been given the name Canto, meaning the principle form of division in a long poem. I immediately set out to write my first book of poems but found my fine motor skills needed time to develop.

I spent my first days getting to know my grandfather, an exceedingly gentle and interesting man. On the third day he was killed by a coronary. I distinctly remember the wake, the endless Hail Marys, the meaningful mourning. When it came time, my father carried me up for the viewing of the body.

I squinted deep at my grandfather looking for secrets, but I found only questions. Why are we made to be expressionless? Should we not be made to look disappointed, or angry? Why, in our caskets, are we not placed in fetal position?

Four days in and our little poodle with the unfortunate name of Jacques, after the famous sea explorer, drowned in the plastic kiddie pool. I was the only one comfortable enough with death to bury him near the swing set. Death comes at us, or death comes from in us, it depends, that is all.

ITEM

Man in bookstore finds pile of brown hair smashed in book, purchases book. Man rides horse home. Rides the back off that horse home. Man bounces on careening horse across rough landscape. Horse slides into corral, dust clouds. Man slips off horse's back, looks in satchel, book still there. Man runs fingers through hair. Man rubs bad bruise on leg. Man strides toward house. Man trips on way up stairs, knocks out front tooth. Man bleeds on porch, hand to face. Horse whinnies. Woman breaks wood out back. Woman snaps branch over knee. Branch splinters. Woman smells wood in arms while walking inside. Woman sees man at table, blood on towel, hand to mouth. Woman looks at man. Man looks at woman. Woman stokes fire with wood. Woman takes man's hand from mouth, looks in mouth, sighs. Man tongues hole. Woman steps out on porch. Horse whinnies. Woman looks for tooth, finds tooth, puts tooth in jar, puts jar in satchel. Man strides out back, lifts ax, chops wood. Woman mounts horse. Horse whinnies. Woman rides horse to town. Rides the back off that horse to town. Woman bounces on careening horse, face in mane. Woman enters bookstore, browses shelves. Woman takes jar from satchel, takes tooth from jar, takes book from shelf, puts tooth in book, closes book, puts book on shelf, puts jar in satchel. Woman rides horse home. Man chops wood. Man lifts ax. Man swings ax.

LOLLIPOP LANE

Someone's goddamn kid at the Lollipop Lane has scabies.

I went to pick up my four-year-old daughter from the daycare center after work as usual. Patricia put her hand on my shoulder and said she needed to speak with me in private. She said there was a slight problem with one of the children.

Patricia's hand was powdery. Her sleeves were rolled up and there were bits of dried plaster stuck in her arm hair. She led me away from the children.

I was thinking, "Who is messing with my daughter now?"

Chelsea is not well liked among her peers. I think it has to do with the outfits she chooses to wear, frilly red tutus and whatnot.

"One of the children has come down with what we believe to be, scabies," sang Patricia, smug-like, as though talking to a toddler. Her dusty white fingers were still on my shoulder leaving traces on my blue blouse.

"Scabies?" I said to her.

"Scabies is caused from an infestation of the skin by the human itch mite." She said this as though it had happened before, as though she had done her research.

"I know what scabies are...is," I said.

My face felt hot. Patricia's cakey hand massaged my shoulder.

She gave me a well-rehearsed look and continued. "The mite burrows into the upper layer of the skin where it lives and lays eggs."

I wanted my daughter. I wanted to take her by her tiny hand and get the hell out of there.

"Now, it's usually spread by direct, skin-to-skin contact, and they can lay dormant for months. So we're going to have to close Lollipop Lane for a while."

'A while?' I was thinking, 'What am I going to do with Chelsea? My mother-in-law is a borderline psychotic and I cannot take time off from the ceramics testing facility without facing serious penalties on my pay.'

"I realize this is difficult," said Patricia, placing her other hand on my other shoulder. "We'll call you when we know the coast is clear."

We went back into the room. The children all occupied themselves in various pockets. At one table Jim Cronson's kid was licking what appeared to be rubber cement off a table, next to him Sarah Marshal's kid plucked and ate the raw macaroni from her greeting card. Tom Watson's kid sat on the floor crying and Frank Arthur's kid squatted silently in the corner with his hands down his pants. They all looked up at me, and a chill bristled my body.

Chelsea, who had apparently been gluing sequins to her face, came bounding up to me, "Mommy!"

When she reached for a hug I turned away from her, "Let's go," I said.

I felt nauseated buckling her into her car seat, my skin pricked with goose bumps. She kissed my cheek and when she wasn't looking, I wiped it on my sleeve. At home I sat clear across the table and watched her eat yogurt in silence, and after she went to bed, I set the house on fire. I sat in the car watching the house glow from inside until it erupted in an unbelievable blaze. The next day I rolled down the window and listened to the blackened ruins hiss and pop in the morning silence.

CARL JUNG BUYS BEANS

"Excuse me sir," said the cashier lady, "do you have your Price Chopper shopper card?"

"No," he said, hardly able to hear himself.

Two cans of beans moved down the belt.

The two of them standing there became something more of themselves together. He bit his lip and prematurely punched in his debit numbers. He felt something beneath his shoe, a hard candy of some kind. It sickened him and he kicked at it but it stuck to the floor. A faint smell of onions moved around them.

The cashier lady felt tired. Her cat had died two days ago, her father was becoming more and more despondent at the home, her car had begun to backfire, and it was getting towards the end of her shift. Her fingers had long curved nails that click-clacked on the keys as she typed in a code for the beans.

Her nails transfixed him. He had never seen nails so long and round. 'How does she manage with those things?' he thought. 'How does she change the station on her radio, or tie her shoes, or play her guitar, or wipe?' he thought. He felt stupid for thinking these things—'her guitar?' He closed his eyes and subtly mouthed the words, shut up.

As subtle as his gesture was, she had noticed.

The beans were not to be found in the system. She pulled the receiver from the wall and her voice boomed throughout the store, "Can I get a price check on thirteen?"

She watched him shift his weight from one foot to the other. She watched him stare down at her hands. She looked at the customers waiting in line behind him: a woman holding a child, a man in a green parka, hood pulled up, and a teenager with pink hair and rings in his nose and ears. She scanned the items on the belt: a chicken, a gallon of milk, Melba toast, 'What the fuck is Melba toast?' she thought. Greek yogurt, Coors Light, corn flakes, Mr. Pibb, brownie mix, tuna fish.

He bent forward, trying to get a closer look. On each nail was an extraordinarily delicate painting of a tiny scene: white horses grazed in gray fields that seemed to undulate in a breeze on the slope of a mountain. The light was such that the moon was still out, but the sun was just coming up. The grass was carefully lined so that almost every blade looked drawn in and dewy, and over the field, a soft fog had begun to gather and form.

DIAL 7 FOR ROBERTO

I just don't feel the same way, he said after my trembling confession. I stuffed the rest of the pancetta into my mouth and chewed it. It tasted like sweat.

It's just too fast for me, I mean, too soon, he said.

I winced, opened my phone and dialed 7 for Roberto. It's a go, I said, and closed it with a slap.

He ignored this and stared into the trees sipping his white wine. I ordered yet another water, I was very thirsty. We did not speak.

When I saw Roberto approaching from behind him

I nearly choked on the water I sipped, taking it down the wrong pipe. Roberto pulled an old T-shirt over his face to blind him, knocking over his chair and dragging him backwards toward the white van. He writhed and screamed and scratched at Roberto's huge hands.

There was a slight commotion on the patio, men stood from their chairs and gasped loudly.

What have I done? I thought.

When the van screeched away the men lowered themselves slowly to their chairs, blinking at one another.

Goodbye, I whispered to the remaining Brie, or in no particular direction, goodbye, I said.

The waiter came and asked in an accent if I knew the man who took my husband. That, I said to him, was not my husband. That, I said to him, pointing to the knocked over chair, was unrequited love. That, I said with greater emphasis, pointing at the sky, was unreciprocated feelings.

The waiter's black mustache twitched. He fell to his knees and wept onto my pant leg, wetting it. The men, startled, stood again, scraping the legs of their chairs against the pavement and dropping their forks on their plates.

Please, I said, you are wetting my slacks.

The waiter stood slapping his hands to his face and running, a little dramatically I thought, off the patio and into the kitchen.

The men stood slightly bent over their tables, over their pastrami sandwiches and cold beet salads, watching the swinging kitchen door. When it ceased to swing, they lowered themselves again uneasily to their chairs, tucked the napkins back into their collars, tossed the ties over their shoulders, and lifted their forks with unsteady fingers.

THE SUN

The sun spun. The sun went on spinning, as usual. The sum of its spinning being very much worth the effort. The sun spun and spun, the sum being so much worth the effort. The sun was spent. Was spun. So spun up it was spun out. But there it was, still spinning. Around the sun, stars. Though not really. If the sun were scaled down to the size of a period on a page   .   the closest star would be eight miles away. If the earth were scaled down to the size of a period on a page   .   the sun would be roughly the size of an orange. For the sake of the sun let's imagine the closest star, so far away. We can all imagine the sound the sun makes. The low pulsations. The droning grumble. In truth the space around the sun is vacuous. In truth, space is vacuous. So, no, no sound. However, we can all imagine what it would be, should we be able to hear it. A deep oscillation. Supposedly without the sun we would not live. But there it is spinning, and so live we do.

In the beginning we all contain the spongy hearts of reptiles. We detect the sun the way a light sensitive blind person senses a soft orangeness. We do not know what it is to breathe and so do not desire it. We do not desire. We simply absorb fluids and wait, though we have no concept of time. We have no concept. We do not know down from up, we are unaware of gravity. Some of us listen to a muffled tinkling in a strangely melodic pool around us. Most of us hear an occasional dense and desperate moan, we hear large and rhythmic thumpings and a sort of, a kind of rushing noise. We can distinguish between noises. We move, at first involuntarily, stretching and flexing, kicking and punching. We squirm. We move through periods of activity and inactivity. We sleep. We sleep soundly. We sleep so soundly we dream.

CHiPS

I shook the shelf, which clattered on the floorboards. My sister clambered over the couches. My father watched CHiPS on TV and in the kitchen my mother caught fire.

I heard the scream and stopped making noise. My father turned down the volume and sat forward on the chair. My sister hid behind the couch. Smoke flitted through the seams of the kitchen door. We were afraid to go into the kitchen. I could smell burning fabric and maybe hair. I could hear wailing and stomping.

My father stood up and turned off the TV. He stood

there with the remote in his hand. My sister pushed herself under the couch as far as she could go, an arm and a leg sticking out.

I went to the kitchen door and opened it a crack. I could see my mother, flailing around, whipping dishtowels. Other things had caught fire too. The curtains were on fire, the plants in the windows were on fire, the stove was on fire, even the floor was on fire. My mother's dress was burning and her hair and her hands were burning. I could feel the heat of the fire on my forehead. I could feel the heat on my lips and cheeks.

I knew my father was standing behind me. He pulled the door quietly closed. He was crying; his hands were shaking.

"Who wants ice cream?" he whimpered.

"I do I do!" came my sister's voice from under the couch.

We left quickly out the front door. No one said a word on the way to the parlor. No one said a word in the parlor. I had peanut butter and chocolate on a sugar cone and my sister had strawberry on a cake cone.

When we got home my mother was sitting on the couch watching CHiPS on TV.

The house smelled like smoke and wet ash. The birds had all been let out of their cages. They flashed blue and green overhead.

THE END

The shovel head had broken off in the mud. I flung the handle over my head, spun it deep into the woods. There was to be no burying here. I took the animal by its leg and dragged it through the leaves and over the knotty roots of trees. It was too heavy so I stopped and emptied it of its insides, combing them out through the hole I had made in its stomach. I left them there in a pile for flies to have their way with.

I live in a home half submerged in the earth. My home faces west for the evening sun to fill. Through the wall at the back of my home I can hear the heavy earth moving. Worms

I think. On the roof I've planted lima beans. At a distance from the house I roast pigs in a pit I've dug. They are delicious when glazed.

A few months back I lost a mare and two roasting pigs to a man, said he'd been out hunting fox and misfired. I squinted one eye and took aim at him with the shovel. He broke forward, toes in the mud. Ran straight into that old dead pine out back and kept on running.

That tree fell finally yesterday. It fell so hard it seemed to shake the animals from the ground and from the trees around it.

Termites devoured most of the shed. Feral cats devoured the field mice, and then I found the cats devoured. I found them deflated and eyeless, tucked in deep around the footing of the barn.

The tractor wouldn't start. I oiled it and pulled at its parts. It took two tow oxen to tug it out into the field. In the field I found what remained of my father: a few dusty smoking pipes and a gray flannel jacket. This is what he had left in a box before tucking in his shirttails and heading far off to someplace else. I dumped them in the field that day and sat so long in the tall grass crying I was burnt crisp by the sun. Had to succumb to the latherings of Ms. June's burn salve. Rubbed it all up and down me. I had ceased to cry at that point. I teased Ms. June about what else she could do with that old burn salve. She scowled and slapped my chest so hard her white handprint lingered there till the burn cooled and disappeared.

THE PROFESSOR, HIS PUPIL,
AND HIS PUPPY PICKLE

A pensive professor sits at a small kitchen table with his finger in a bowl of hot roiling grits. At his foot sits his puppy Pickle. Pickle sits lapping up the puddle of grits that the professor earlier spilt.

"Anxiety," says the professor to his dog, who glances up at him imploringly. "Anxiety, Pickle, is at the root of everything."

Pickle barks sharply as though in response to the professor's rumination.

In a jar on the table is a small blue betta fish swimming in circles. The professor taps quietly on the jar and the fish tries in vain to attack the tip of his finger.

There is a blunt knock on the door. The professor lurches from his seat and walks to the door, shuffling his shoes. Through the peephole the professor can make out the white face of his pupil. He does not wish to see his pupil and so holds his breath. He continues to squint through the peephole as his pupil knocks again. It is very quiet. In the back of the room he can hear the radiator heat ticking out from the pipes. Rolling his eyes he glances down at Pickle imploringly.

"Professor, I know you're in there," says his pupil in a high-pitched voice.

"You son of a bitch," whispers his pupil.

The professor frowns, only inches away. Pickle whimpers and falls into one of his spasms. The pupil watches the dog's trembling shadow through the slit under the door. He twists the doorknob. He straightens his tie, "You son of a bitch."

The pupil takes the elevator down to the parking garage where he sits in his Porsche finishing the last few fries that had fallen loose in the bag.

He slams his palm on the steering wheel and drives, a little recklessly, to the Drug Emporium for Sucrets, as his throat has been bothering him for decades.

Standing quietly in the checkout line, the pupil runs into the poet Peter Gizzi who mistakes him for another person then quickly attempts to sell him a book that he produces from out of what seems like nowhere.

IT IS MY UNDERSTANDING

It is my understanding that dogs root through our garbage at night. A muzzle stuck in a plastic sack might discover the discarded wrappings of the things we survive on.

Would it in fact be inconsiderate of me to point out the trepidations I have over such things? These dogs could in fact expose who we are to our neighbors, the Havershamps.

Would it in fact be insensitive of me to speak too much of these dogs to my family? My family, so frightened of animals, especially those of the canine variety? I take great pride in my enormous capacity for sensitivity.

It is my understanding that these dogs run in packs and should be carefully watched. It is my understanding that we are not alone on this.

The Havershamps have taken to shooting at the dogs with a rifle. The rifle fires blanks. Personally I find it pointless, though they do scatter, the dogs do scatter in a roundabout sort of way.

These dogs, they do not, will not, touch the recyclables. Nothing of interest in there I suppose.

Personally I do not recycle my recyclables. I find it pointless.

The Havershamps, for instance, build stacks of boxes and bottles, plasticy things, slices of cardboard and crates of containers on the sidewalk. The compost pile behind their house is completely out of control. I have never in my life seen a pile of shit reach that high. The smell is unbearable. Layers of fruit pit, of vegetable rind and coffee ground. Sometimes at night I can hear it shifting under itself. I can hear it give and collapse.

Occasionally I go to the back porch in the evening and sit on the deck chair and smoke a cigarillo and watch the pile steam. I sit on the deck chair and watch the pile sit in their yard.

Last night I saw Mrs. Havershamp in her kitchen window washing dishes. She stopped washing the dishes and stood staring at the heap for some time in the soft orange light of her kitchen. I'd like to get to know Mrs. Havershamp better. My god she is lovely. There is something simple in the way she washes dishes that destroys the way I feel about everything else in the world.

STUCK

(FOR MY FATHER)

I thought I could fit my head between the slats of my bunk bed ladder. As it turned out I was right, but could not pull it out again. I tried squeezing and wiggling. I tried prying with my fingers. My ears felt warm and bruised. They felt ten times their normal size. I gave up and cried for a while.

I stuck out my tongue to taste the ladder. It tasted like sand from the playground and I spit onto my sister's pillow.

I put my hands in my pants.

I stood there hunched over with my head in the wood ladder till my dad came home and unscrewed one of the planks. My dad stripped the screw holes getting me out of there. He pulled the ladder apart, leaned the plank against the wall, and stood looking at me with welled-up eyes as though this were bound to happen again.

My dad had to lift me that night into the top bunk. I did not sleep well, thinking I would never come back down.

GIRL, MAKES SENSE TO ME

Tom, during lunch, asked me to join his boy band. I took another bite of my tuna fish sandwich.

We are emergency operators. Most of our time is spent tucked away in half-cubicles with headsets making permanent indentions in our otherwise well-coiffed hair.

DialaLife is a mid-level medical alert company near the highway on a strip of land owned by the airport. All day long we hear jet engines screaming through the leak-stained ceiling panels.

When a phone rings we push a button and recite the

sentence: "Hello, this is your emergency operator, do you need help?!" Throughout the Center, this line echoes like a cultish mantra. Most of the time we answer calls from lonely old folks who just want someone to talk to.

Henry Tarwhip from Pike's Bluff, Georgia, has called in every afternoon for three years now.

"Hello Henry, this is your emergency operator, do you need help?!"

Henry is always disappointed if he reaches a male operator and will continue to push his alert button until he gets a girl.

We are instructed to ask these casual callers how the weather is in their part of the country and end the call pleasantly. We are not allowed to chitchat with the customers.

One call in every seven is an actual emergency. For these we find out the problem—heart attack, stroke, broken hip— and keep the customer on one line while pushing another button to call an ambulance. It is often the spouse of the customer calling in to tell us the customer has died. It is protocol not to cry during these intense calls, though I am a silent crier so I just let go.

With each call we must fill out a Customer Alert Form detailing the time, name, location, and reason for call.

I spend my time between calls writing lyrics on the backs of the blank forms.

Tom somehow got a hold of my song titled *Girl, Makes Sense to Me*. The song touches on my feelings surrounding the initial attraction to, further wooing of, seven-month relationship with, and inevitable breakup by Samantha Lafayette.

All of my songs touch on this subject.

So during lunch, Tom sits down at my table with his steaming Styrofoam cup of Ramen and says, "Listen, I have a serious proposition for you. I'd like you to join my boy band." I have *the* look, he says. We need a *bad boy* member, he says. I have the *bad boy* look? I ask. Yes man, yes you do, look at your hair, *and* you can write. With this he slaps *Girl, Makes Sense to Me* on the table. I take a bite of my tuna fish sandwich.

Listen, Tom, I don't know, I've never sung in front of anyone before, I say.

Just come in for one rehearsal, tonight after work, says Tom.

As it turns out, I also have *the* voice because at rehearsal the other guys were like, whoa, oh man, this is like, fate.

The truth is, Tom trusted me to carry the band. Now it's too late. My second solo album is due out in a month. The first one was well received. Tom died of a bath salt overdose two years ago. Gary came out, went straight again, then back out. Vinnie works at a post office in rural Nebraska. And Turner had two kids, gained three hundred pounds, and checked himself into a facility.

NORMAN MAILER

Despite the common conception, goldfish have reasonably good memories.

A week ago I sat on my kitchen counter swirling my finger around in Norman Mailer's bowl. I poked him in the eye on accident and he hasn't looked at me the same since. It's been an entire week and he still sort of squints at me as he swims.

Norman Mailer is a feeder fish. This means he was bred and raised in a pet store as live food for something else.

A week ago my boyfriend left me, said he had been reading too much Norman Mailer, said he had a lot to think about.

My psychiatrist said I had misdirected animosity and that it was neither my boyfriend, Keith, nor our goldfish, Norman Mailer, that I wanted to blame, but my mother.

I've decided to leave my psychiatrist. Not because of what she said, but because she has cerebral palsy and I just can't take her seriously with her hands all pretzeled up like that. I'll tell her that I've been reading too much Norman Mailer and that I have a lot to think about.

My psychiatrist does not think I am funny. I am always trying to make little jokes but she just raises her penciled-in eyebrows and rotates her hands.

I am sitting on my kitchen counter swirling my finger around in Norman Mailer's bowl again. I have to go to work in an hour. I work at the airport where time passes in short intervals, from one flight to the next, in the comings and go-ings of people. I have never even been on an airplane. I am terrified of the long descent before a horrific plane crash, terrified of what I might think about.

Every night I pick out a passenger from the crowd and imagine him on the plane, listening to headphones and sip-ping a ginger ale. I imagine sitting in the seat next to him, imagine the scent of peanuts, the slight rumble of the engine, the small sounds of the other passengers. I imagine holding his hand in mine and looking out the window at the world so far below me.

THE TURNING OF EVENTS

No matter how often I try, I cannot for the life of me get it together.

I remember once a little while ago thinking, 'How have I gotten myself into this, into this mess that I'm in?'

The turning of events was how it happened, the precious and terrible turning of events. How odd how that sometimes happens. How quick the turn. From one thing into another.

I remember once I tried turning back and away from the turning of events, if only to get myself out of the mess I was in. I tried staying in one place and staying still. I turned off all the lights and locked all the doors and held my breath for as long as I could. I closed my eyes and cleared my thoughts for as long as I could. Events continued to turn. There were events turning, events I wasn't even aware of.

I became aware then that in order to deal with the turning of events one must get it together.

Now I sit here and once again try to get it together.

Get it together, I say to myself.

Deal, I say.

One of these days I'll get it together. One of these days I'll deal and I'll have my turn too. Say what you will, one of these days I will turn, and see in my turn the rest of it, everywhere, all of it everywhere, behind me.

URGEBIRGE

What you need to know about Lehman is, he loves the opera, loves the drama, the flamboyant costume, and the ballsy orchestration of it. He is especially fond of singing it, mostly to himself, in particular, *Orpheus and Eurydice*, by Christoph von Gluck. He belts the sound of this story over the cliffs of the Ural Mountains in the eastern slopes of Russia while pitching his tent for the night. His barrel-chested voice is the only available sound in the region.

Lehman has made a mistake: There is a gap in the road. The horses will not cross this divide; they lift their muzzles to the sky and try tugging the cart back down the mountain. Peter, the assistant, sits in the dirt scratching a swollen mosquito bite on his ankle. Lehman pulls at the rope with one arm and swats the horses with the other.

Now they sit ruefully at a crevice.

Catherine the Great had invited Lehman to move to St. Petersburg as Professor of Chemistry and Official Director of the Imperial Museum. He packed his things in a hurry, absentmindedly leaving behind his bronzed fingernail clippers, as well as the can opener, anxious to catch the next train out of town.

Having forgotten to pack a proper opener, Johann Gottlob Lehman splits open a can of beans with a sharp piece of shale. Most of the beans spill out black on the gray rocks. The cliffs he sits on fall away at his feet, down crags and snowy patches and into a place where the hills quietly meet. He lifts the mangled can to his mouth; beans spill out onto his ruffled cravat. At his feet, a satchel of explosives stews in the sun.

"The placement of rocks on or below the earth's surface is not random, rather it reflects a specific geological history," he says smugly to himself.

Lehman buys time: One evening, over tin cups of brandy, Lehman delicately coins the term, *Urgebirge*, or primitive rocks.

One morning, Lehman wakes early and skips toward the cliff's edge to urinate. He watches over his shoulder as the pack-mule rubs itself against the wall of rock near the tent behind him and notices the bright orange mineral deposits crumbling over the mule's back. He laughs as he carefully takes a sample and calls it Siberian Red Lead, then stands, singing its name over the cliff, again and again.

This mineral would later be identified as the newest element, chromium. Even though it took up to two years to transport the mineral from the Beresof mines via pack mule to the sophisticated peoples of western Europe, Siberian Red Lead became popular as a paint pigment for the likes of Joe Turner, Bill Blake, Joan Ingres, and Gene Delacroix to name only a few. A stunning bright yellow paint made from the mineral ('that of a thousand burning barn fires' as the composer Nick Paganini once remarked), became an increasingly fashionable color for the garish carriages of the nobility in England and France.

Lehman conducts an experiment: Happy in his position as Professor Director, he retires early one evening to his laboratory in St. Petersburg to test more chromium samples. Lehman's concoction of arsenic, chromium, and gunpowder results in an impressively brilliant yellow explosion that renders him absolutely no longer alive.

PREDATION

That bird was fucking huge, most definitely flightless. It ran awkwardly forward swinging its heavy head by its long neck. It frothed at the mouth, or beak, as it were. It tried to lift off several times flapping those tiny wings against its big featherless body. Hopeless. It burned a lot of energy running back and forth trying to fly. Eventually, that bird burned up all of its energy. When it died, we ate it.

Then there was that cat. Or at least we think it was a cat. Except it had these strange thick claws and these long, long arms and no ears, and it hung upside down from a tree branch. We watched it from below for a while and nothing much happened. It moved so slowly. At one point I'm pretty sure it was asleep. Sim said someone should climb up there and get it, but it was Sim who saw it first so we made him do it. His thighs got all scratched inching up the tree. When he got to the branch he clung on and shook it like crazy. It took a lot of shaking but eventually the cat slipped off. When it hit the ground it died and we ate it.

Some time went by and Sim spotted this thing watching us from the bushes. Sim was by far our best spotter. We all got up from the fire too quick and it bolted backward, turned, and bared some serious fucking teeth. It had this wild red nose with sky blue lines on the edges, a yellow beard, and mean yellow eyes too close together.

This thing was terrifying. I dropped my potatoes and went straight fetal. Sim speared it and we ate it but I was ridiculed all through dinner. Sim nearly choked on the *meat* of this thing he was laughing so hard. When I walked out this morning everyone acted scared and went fetal, then held their bellies laughing. I know I will never hear the end of it.

SHIFTING AND
PLUMMETING

The two boys sat atop the refrigerator, swinging their legs, banging their heels and laughing with their wide mouths open. One sucked at a wine bottle, spitting zinfandel across the kitchen and onto the shimmering hair of the party guests who bobbed below in the darkness. The other smoked at a cigarette.

The idea was to pass for a desirable human being: charming, available, smart and funny, possibly gifted, even good-looking.

The idea was to disguise what was less than desirable,

socially disabled, socially unstable, grotesque even, even pitiful, even frank.

Well, below them two girls of relative appearance and age adjusted magnetic letters on the freezer to spell out suggestive slogans. Their arms twisted about, brushing against one another, warming one another.

Music, when called music, remains notched into a category reserved for listeners. This room, this kitchen, was filled with people lost to listening, beyond the act. Entirely too focused on each other's eyes and movements, too focused on balancing, on gravity, too focused on not toppling into one another, on bobbing and looking pained, looking serious in the cheeks. This music was not throbbing as so many would have it but shifting and plummeting.

One of the two girls tugged at one of the two boys' coarse pant leg and down he went, over the refrigerator and into the bobbing blackness.

The other boy's face darkened and sank in and away from itself. He stopped swinging his legs, banging his heels. He stopped spitting the wine and he turned in on himself. He stood, as best he could, atop the refrigerator, ducking down to avoid the ceiling, and tossed the bottle into the dark bobbing sound. He folded his arms over his chest and dropped headfirst into it. He dropped headlong into it and disappeared.

"TELL ME WITH WHOM YOU WALK AND I WILL TELL YOU WHO YOU ARE"

My father ordered a vaquero from amazon.com. He was grilling flank steaks on the back patio when I asked him what that was. He poked at the steaks with a long sharp-pronged fork and without looking up at me he whispered, "It's a Mexican cowboy."

We lived in a small cape with black gables jutting from the roof on a quiet, neighborly cul-de-sac. We did not own a horse, or cattle, or anything I could think of to justify ordering a vaquero.

I looked past my father and into the neighbor's living

room window. I could see Mr. Havershamp sprawled out on the sofa watching Sesame Street.

A moth tumbled out of our light fixture, and my father waved it away with the pronged fork. I looked beyond the patio and spotted one of my red hot-wheels half buried in the mulch. "What fer?" I asked, trying to be funny but with little self-confidence. My father slowly looked up from the grill and at our house. His eyes were glassy and blood-shot. "Go tell your mother the steaks are ready."

Over the next week my parents made up a cot for the vaquero in my room despite my many protests. When he arrived, I was watching from my bedroom window. He stepped down from the UPS truck in full gear: ostrich skin boots with spurs, furry angora chaps, rusty mascada around his neck and a black hat. My father yelled from the stairs, "Get down here, pronto!" The vaquero's hand was heavy and coarse when we shook, and mine was mashed potatoes.

He slept in his clothes that night, chaps and all, hat pulled down over his face. I lay completely still, my heart like a rabbit's, until the sun came up.

This went on for years until I went off to college. He never said a word. I'd find him at the kitchen table with my father in the mornings chewing plugs of tobacco. I'd go to pour Frosted Flakes in a bowl and I could feel him watching me from under the brim of his hat. At school the kids taunted me, "Yippee-yo-ki-ay!" When prodded at PTA meetings, my father became defensive and reserved about his need for a vaquero.

In the end, because of the vaquero I suppose, I am more of a man than I would have been otherwise.

SHE THOUGHT

She sat on the front porch sipping chicken soup. In the road, two small boys latched arms and jigged, or shuffled, jig-like. They are like munchkins, she thought. Like mayors of the Munchkin City. They represent the Lollipop Guild, she thought.

This thought made her laugh. The boy's shuffling left a pillowing trail of dust and they were gone.

She poured the rest of her chicken soup into her dog's dish. The dog had been dead a week now. She looked down at the soup in the dish from the stoop where she sat. She looked down a bit longer and dipped a finger in it to swirl it around.

Her dog still lay in the grass, its skin draped over its bones. Like the sheet they slide over a body's face, she thought. Like the skin on an old lady's hand. Like a carpet left out in the rain, she thought. The ground around the dog was swelling with mushrooms.

Lately she had been feeling a great since of urgency, like strange water had been slowly rising her entire life and now it had reached her chin.

"SINCE WE ARE LOST,
LET'S GO TO THE RIVER"

Father tied a forty-foot rope from the doorknob of the house to the barn handle out back. The rope led us all the way across the yard down a few snow-beaten slopes. Nothing but snow out there. That coarse half-frozen rope between our hands was the only thing that kept us on track in that impossible white stretch.

The blizzards were bad back then. Without that rope, you'd take a wrong turn and end up frozen solid in one of the many fields surrounding our property. I remember that old barn like I was standing in it now. Horse pee soaked up into the planks past the hay and vermin. That smell was atrocious. Those horses, navigating under heinous conditions in zero visibility; it seemed to pull them out of their wits. You'd be riding to fetch firewood in all that snow and they'd start kicking up and circling. They'd nearly throw you, which would mean a certain end. So father made us special reins from the small intestine of a dead steer we found while hunting. These were long enough to tie around our waists a few times and stronger than steel cable. That way if you got thrown, you'd at least be dragged home through the snow.

One day I was out in the forest hunting jackrabbit and I heard howling. The trees were so plastered with snow I could barely make them out. I followed the sound with my rifle ready and found the most unspeakable blood trail I'd ever seen. It started at a tripped bear trap, and what looked to be the gnarled torn foot of a boy. The amount and color of blood against all that white was a sight to see. My horse spooked but we kept on.

Sure enough, at the end of the trail was the neighbor's kid Thomas, foot chewed straight through. He'd crawled about forty feet and stopped when the last of his blood left him. His face was nearly as white as the snow. I slung him over my horse and when I went to fetch his foot I found a skinny coyote tugging it from the trap. I went to shoot the animal but thought that foot would do that old coyote better than it would young Thomas here, so I let it be.

BLOW THE MAN DOWN

I fucked a Greek fisherman. She was gorgeous you know. She spoke of Hume on the boat, holding her long fishy fingers in the dark green water.

From where we sat in the sea, we could smell the industrial revolution taking place up the rocky shoreline.

"Experience and observation," she said, "I am bound up in it."

She twisted her long black hair in her fists; the water ran dark green from them, down and over her waxy chest.

It used to be I'd part ways with the things I'd wanted. Say

I'd met this fisherman a few years earlier. Say I decided she was the right girl for me, and off I'd go, away from her and all the things I'd thought before.

On the boat I looked at her and my senses said everything. She snatched a carp up from the sea with one long arm. The fish tossed in the boat.

"He reminds me of you," she said looking down at the gasping carp.

She put her fingers in the carp's mouth as if to calm it. It seemed to calm, and lie still.

I could tell something was off. I accused her of taking another man when it was I who had taken another woman.

"Back it up," she said,

"Shut it down," she said.

She stood and spread her legs wide in the boat and rocked it back and forth.

She capsized the boat and I nearly drowned. Saved by a handsome windsurfer who went by the name of Dartanion.

While I recovered in the hospital they got together, my Greek fisherman and Dartanion. They careened, fell fast and into the various pits and parts of one another. Something in the way they meshed, the one into the other made sense I suppose.

Over time they became inseparable. Much like the sea. This sea is inseparable. If docked near the foot of it one might make out the gray line of my dark skiff lilting along the horizon, but no, it's getting darker, darker and more difficult to see. I've found a way to keep myself at a distance from the lurching of it cutting and tying nets for fishing purposes. My hands are twisting the wet cords into nets right now. I run my hands through a cycle of scrubbing every day to rid them of, well, to rid them.

The Greek fisherman's hands were symmetrical and spindly.

I recall the shape of her, curled up in the skiff after sex. She watched me, afterwards, all the pink tendernesses stolen from her. She twitched at the end and rubbed one socked foot against mine to satisfy an itch that had likely been bothering her the whole time.

IN THE MUD, IN HER ARMS

I shot the animal near the river. It struggled for some time, whining and twisting in the mud. I had bought the animal at an auction. The animal was ugly but inexpensive.

My sister really loved the animal. My sister loved to ride the animal, though she was probably too big for it.

The animal once ate my favorite pair of pants. Just took the pants in its big mouth and ate them.

It's not that I hate the animal. It's not that the animal has done me wrong, has done anything an animal shouldn't do. Sure, the animal smelled bad, sure it ate things that did not belong to it, things that belonged to me. I do not blame the animal for what it was. It was only an animal after all.

Now the animal is dead in the mud and I am the one who shot it. If my sister should see this, see the animal dead in the mud like this, she would probably cry. My sister would probably hold the animal, in the mud, in her arms, and cry.

I do not want my sister to see that I have shot the animal. I do not want my sister to see me standing here by the river, see me standing here in my wading boots, with my rifle, with my fake mustache and my basket of rabbits.

Now that the animal is dead, I can go about my business, now that the animal is dead.

IT'S ONLY A
MATTER OF TIME

She sat next to me on the log prying open a can of beans. The fire spit and flicked and lit up her face with its orange light.

"Someday we'll both be dead together," she said to me, grinning at the flames and then down at the beans. "One day, someday, you will be dead, and I will too already be dead," she said, looking me in the eyes.

I looked back at her questioningly.

I touched her cheek with the tips of my fingers.

"One day we'll both be dead and won't that be nice?" she asked, looking up at the trees and probably out past them into the stars. She sighed and lifted a forkful of beans to her mouth, "No matter what, one day we'll be dead together," she said, just before taking the bite and chewing.

She finished chewing and smiled at me, "No matter what, one dead we'll be day together, I mean dead!" she said.

She laughed shortly and shook her head smiling. She put the fork in the can and her hand on my leg.

"One day... someday, we'll both be dead, and won't that be nice?" she asked and pinched my knee.

She sat for a moment looking at her hand on my knee.

"Sometime maybe we'll both die?" she seemed to be asking the trees around us.

"One of these days..." she said under her breath.

She reached for the bag of marshmallows and the stick she had sharpened earlier. She handed me a marshmallow, and we both stuck one on the end of our sticks. We sat listening to the fire for some time, turning our marshmallows gently to brown them, watching them bubble and smoke. I watched her squint into the fire.

"Ok, so someday we'll both die and ha! Dead!" She said.

Her marshmallow hissed as it caught fire and she blew it out.

TO BE READ ALOUD
WITH A LISP

The teapot steamed and stood steaming for some time as a teapot will do without the assistance of someone lifting it from the stove where it sits. I stood up from the position I was in to pour a cup and scalded my friggin finger. I ran water over it. I ran it under and over it. I blew on it until it was cool enough. There were no cups to put the tea in so I left it in the pot where it sat. Where I left it, it changed a bit, it steeped a bit. It changed into something more fit for it. I sipped at it from the spout. I tasted it.

It turned out to be too hot and I dropped it, I dropped

it and it spilled and scalded the puppy. The puppy yelped and slipped from where it stood. The puppy slid down to the tiles and sat there staring up.

I took the tap in my mouth to cool my tongue. I turned on the tap to test the temperature and it too turned out to be too hot. Shit. I thought. I am so sick of this. I thought.

I went to see if some mail had come. I looked into the slit and slid open the letter to see what it said, this is it:

Sir, Still speculating on the size of your studio, it is speciously spatial, especially special and spatial. Specifically not stereotypical, but typically specific, so seemingly seamless is it. Its craft is explicit in its expertise. Though they wish to ship it in the Pacific. So just skip it.

Sincerely, PP and Stern Attorneys At Law.

I wasn't sure what to make of it. I speculated. I posited. The studio was still for sale, still situated for sale so far as I could tell. Perhaps someone wanted it, wanted to purchase it and ship it in the Pacific. But skip it? Perhaps I should seek out this PP and Stern Law Office and see.

Soon I sought out the office. The office was spacious. I saw the secretary at her desk.

"May I please speak to PP, or Stern?" I asked.

"Certainly sir," she said speaking up at me.

She pressed a spot and PP sounded softly through the speaker system.

"This is PP," he said.

"PP there is a Mr..." she said staring up at me.

"Mr. Sploop," I said.

"A Mr. Sploop here to see you sir, something about a studio for sale." When PP stepped from his office I saw that he was short and pleasantly plump.

"Mr. Sploop, I presume," he said, shaking my hand. He spoke with a lisp.

"Yes," I said, "I wish to speak with you about this post, the subject of which is my studio for sale."

"Oh, the studio on Stapleton Street, yes yes," he said, "suppose I was to say that my clients, the Pattersons, wish to purchase this studio? Suppose I was to say the Pattersons wish to ship it to a place somewhere possibly problematic, specifically speaking, across the Pacific?"

"I must admit, that does seem absurd." I said

"Sir," said P.P. "let us consider at some length, the Myth of Sisyphus."

"The Myth of Sisyphus?" I asked

"Yes, the Myth of Sisyphus. By Camiss, father of the philosophical studies on Existentialism."

"My sweet P.P., I believe it is pronounced Cam-oo."

"Is it?"

"It is."

"If you say so. Anyways, in his famous essay, he relates the situation of Sisyphus to man's futile search for significance."

"I'm listening." I said

"Sisyphus, because of his deceitfulness to Zeus as well as Tartarus who was Death personified, was sentenced to push a sizable stone up a steep slope, only to have it slide down the other side, this, in perpetuity."

"Sounds monstrous," I said.

"Yes, though he says we should picture Sisyphus with a smile on his face."

There was a pause.

"You see?" asked P.P.

I was suspicious, I squinted, I hesitated, and he promptly produced the publication from its place on the shelf. I poked through it and perceived that this was so.

"Yes, I see, I see," I said.

"Brass tacks," he said, "to make matters simple, they wish to pay you a lump sum of seven hundred and seventy seven thousand dollars and sixty six cents (for tax purposes)."

My eyes were luminous. 'That sum is preposterous,' I thought.

"That sum seems perfectly reasonable," I said.

"Then the problem is solved," he said.

He let go his grip, his lips pursed and he spat into his palm. I spat into mine and we shook, smiling.

"Sold," I said.

THE SCAPEGOAT

"You have died of dysentery," said the chief priest to the body, sliding his palm over its eyes to close them.

In the morning, after the burial, the priest performed a ritual, whereby he laid all the sins of the people upon a goat and sent it staggering into the wilderness.

We all watched from the parquet on fold out chairs, sharing blankets and eating grilled cheese sandwiches.

"That's the last we'll see of that old goat," said Muriel almost inaudibly under her breath.

"Perhaps," said the priest loudly from the parapet.

Somehow he had heard Muriel.

"Perhaps," he said again, pointing at her and walking with long strides in our direction.

I nearly choked on my sandwich watching wide-eyed as he approached with his arm outstretched, finger just barely touching the tip of Muriel's nose.

"But were it not for that old goat," he grumbled, "you would no doubt suffer insurmountable afflictions as did the dysenteric you see stretched out before you."

Muriel swallowed loudly and asked for the priest's forgiveness.

Just then Chauncey came stepping over the parapet from the edge of the woods, arms akimbo, hands in fists. He had been gone for weeks on a walkabout. His beard was grizzly and his tights had runs.

We all gasped in unison.

The priest lowered his arm and looked over his shoulder at Chauncey.

"Who does a guy have to do to get a grilled cheese sandwich around here?" said Chauncey with a shit-eating grin.

A pair of buzzards circled, watching us from the sky. We must look so small to those birds, I thought.

An old man scrambled from his chair to hand Chauncey a sandwich, which he quickly shoved into his bearded mouth.

"I've found true happiness out there," he said, mouth full of sandwich, "and I'm going back for it. Now, who's with me?"

We all looked carefully at one another. Muriel curled her lips at the priest. She stood, removing her half of the blanket, folded her chair, and joined Chauncey. The others followed suit, including the priest, who looked defeated with his hooded head hanging. They each stepped over the parapet, and without even a glance back, disappeared into the woods.

APPROPRIATELY HUNGRY

You pace. You pace in the creek, if that's possible. Pants rolled up above your knees, splashing to and fro. There is no food left on the farm and you are starving. Your dog jumps and wags excitedly as you go. He sometimes nips at you in his excitement, splashing along. You have your mother's wig on, your mother who wore wigs to hide the scant hair on her scalp. The wig is wild and blonde, it hangs down over your face.

Where is she now?

Dead and gone.

You are barefoot, your feet are hard and leathery from all the creek pacing you do, back and forth on the pebbly creek bed. In the trees around you possums cling to branches, all playing dead. When you stop pacing your dog splays his front legs out, hoists his wagging haunch in the air, and waits. When you resume pacing so does the dog.

It is fall and the leaves are red, all over the ground, red. There is only one chicken left back on the farm, one chicken and the dog. This leaves you with an occasional egg, when she has an egg, which is rare. It's an occasional egg for you, and peppercorns from the peppercorn tree.

So you pace and wrack your brain about what to do next. You wrack it about where to go next.

Do you eat the dog?

Look at him, he is so dumb.

Should you eat your own foot?

Ha! No.

There is a cut on your leg from a thistle you walked through to get here. It is bleeding into the creek. The possums all cling to their branches and smile. They are all laughing at you no doubt. You can hear their little laughter. You are not dumb.

Possums! How had you not thought of it! You will eat possum with your peppercorned egg!

You reach into the creek bed for a large stone and chuck it up into the branches. You are not a good aim and it clomps down into the water against other stones. You scoop another out and chuck it again, hard up into the branches, knocking red leaves loose.

CHARLES AND RITA

Charles sat squat in the field, hiding from his sister in the Johnson grass. A seed from the raspberry preserves he had eaten for lunch was lodged between his two front teeth. He flossed with a length of grass to remove it. His gums bled and his eyes watered.

Charles? Came the high lemony voice of his sister Rita through the reeds.

Charlie?

Charles watched Rita, her face as blank and pale as an English muffin.

Rita's convulsions were not an uncommon occurrence. Like a small bird she was sent into these movements at the slightest noise. When she stopped, Charles stepped out of the wood, bent down to smell whether she had lost control of her bladder as so often happens. Instead he saw that she was not breathing. He removed the riding gloves from her fragile fingers and kissed her hands shortly before bolting from the bushes and sprinting down the length of Salisbury Road to the old Havershamp place to find help.

Rita, really quite alright, gathered her gloves, lifted the leaves from her white ziggurat hairdo and walked carefully down to the Ropesbad River to select stones for her growing collection.

As Charles approached the outskirts of the Havershamp farm huffing and heaving for air, he saw two men, one charging at the other with what looked to be a hatchet. The latter man pulled a pistol from his haunch and shot the former man in the...neck, maybe? Why? asked the man with the pistol to the man with the hole in his neck. Why in god's name a hatchet? The man with the hole in his neck began to weep, beg forgiveness, and die.

Charles fell on his knees in the mud while hopping the wooden fence. His sobbing was working its way to the surface of his face when the man pointed the long barrel of his pistol at Charles's head, painfully poking at his scalp.

Charles and Rita had a father named James. He was a military surgeon and a violent alcoholic. In the afternoons when he would return home from work, James would take long naps. Charles and Rita were forced to remain silent and stand watch over his body lest someone break in and tamper with it. Rita was always made ill at the stink of vodka rising up from his pores.

Rita had had a second brother named Burt, but their father killed Burt at an early age. Burt cried too often in his basket. James had restrained the tiny boy with one large hand and poured vodka into his mouth with the other until he drowned. This spelled sorrow for Charles, who had been looking forward to playing tricks on his little brother. Now, Charles would not be able to play the tricks. Which made him sad. Depressed, even.

DUTCH

In the afternoon I nanny for a privileged thirteen-year-old boy named Dutch. My first day on the job the mother told me to meet Dutch at his school, to spot him and walk him home without letting his friends become aware of my presence. I was to remain one half-block back and away from the boy and his friends to keep him from embarrassment. Dutch was apparently very sensitive when it came to embarrassment.

I did as I was told, loitering near the bright yellow buses, pretending to search for lost keys. Sure enough, Dutch stepped out with a pack of boys all loosening their ties, bouncing and snapping at each other with their waistcoats. I mistakenly caught his eye and looked at the ground. The moment was short but his disgusted face let me know he knew I was there for him. I stooped and picked up a Now-and-Later wrapper and poked it into my pocket as though it were what I had been searching for.

The boys headed off in the direction of the village. I followed suit, stopping every now and then to observe the withered leaf of a pin-oak tree between the tips of my fingers or to inconspicuously collect the crumpled pieces of notebook paper the boys left in their wake. I unfolded the papers and found filthy drawings crudely sketched in pencil.

One resembled a de'Kooning woman with huge crooked teeth and an enormous vagina. Another depicted a large dog swallowing a naked man whole, the caption read simply: DUMBASS. At the corner of 63rd and Ruffling I picked up another piece of notebook paper and unfolded it to find the words BACK OFF UGLY scratched into its surface; a moment later another that said TOO CLOSE SHITHEAD. And still another that said QUIT STALKING US FREAK-SHOW.

I kept my pace until I was struck on the forehead by a rock. I picked up the same rock and threw it, with everything I had left, at Dutch. I undershot, and hit the window of a parked station wagon. The boys leapt and cheered, flinging their ties into the air. They hoisted Dutch on their shoulders and carried him the rest of the way home.

SO THAT'S THERE?

How odd to think that beyond this wall in a dimly lit room there sits a shirtless man eating a bag of Lays and humming the Care Bears theme song into a webcam. How strange to suppose that on the other side of this other wall a woman in pajama pants molds slices of Wonder bread into self-portraits that sell like hotcakes on Etsy. What a wonder it is to consider the opposite end of this different wall. Behind it a small gathering of dental students from Bangladesh learn to extract teeth from a dummy. Were it not for this other wall we would never know of what went on within it. No, we would always know. On the other side of it a small girl with long black hair and long green eyes colors in forests with crayons. Beyond this one a branch catches fire. Beyond this one my parents are getting a divorce. Beyond this one a couple copulates. Beyond this one a woman watches. This one, a baby is born and dies. This one a teenager sings, I don't know much, but I know I love you to his new girlfriend. This one has no windows but is filled with light. On the other side of this one a man carefully clips his toenails. How weird to think that beyond this wall two women wait for what is bound to be wonderful. And to think—a bowl of spaghetti sits steaming on a perfectly made bedspread.

WILD ASS

It took a long time to tame the wild ass. I warned Polito that it might. He would not listen. The tamed ass was only two hundred dollars more but Polito would not listen.

One of the farm hands, Romero, took a hoof in the back and was permanently paralyzed. Another named Buck was trampled to death while whispering in its oversized ear. The ass dragged a man named Carlos from one end of the corral to the other. Carlos is still in a coma.

One day the grounds keeper, Johann, tried to tame the ass with a bit of sugar cake. The ass bit off the hand of

Johann who now wears a hook where the hand once was. Johann is always at the tavern telling the tale of how the ass took his hand. Polito pulled a muscle, split his skull, and was forced to remove a ruptured spleen. Jesus was drunk and thought he could tame the ass with a song. In the end it took a full two months and twelve men to tame the ass.

The survivors, including myself, are not looking forward to taming the wild pony.

QUALITY TIME

I asked my mom over Christmas sparerib if I was a forcep baby due to the obvious asymmetry of my head. She laughed and scraped the fork on her teeth.

We stayed up late watching *Minute to Win It* and drinking hot cider with rum. The oddly shaped standard poodle stood from where it slept across the room, trotted to where I sat on the couch, and threw up in my lap.

At brunch my grandma fed her boyfriend sausages, massaging them down his trachea. He is ninety-eight, deaf, blind, wheelchair-bound, and if he is feeling particularly like sausages that day, someone has to massage them into him.

Grandma showed us a photo of her boyfriend's family Christmas in 1917. She held one of those butterfly picture frames. On one side was her boyfriend's family photo; a napkin mysteriously covered the other side.

"What's under the napkin, Grandma?" I asked.

"Oh you don't want to see that!" she said.

"What is it?" I said, feigning impatience.

Under the napkin was a photo of Grandma in her twenties. "Oh it's just me when I was younger, wasn't I beautiful?" she said, pulling the napkin away with a flourish.

After brunch we watched Fox news while Grandma force-fed everyone oddly shaped pieces of fire candy with her fingers. At one point she gripped my knee, got right in my face and said, "The other day Lou stopped moving and I thought he had passed so I leaned in like this and said, Just go to the angels honey! Just go to the angels!"

Apparently Grandma pulled my terrified girlfriend aside and asked her if she believed in angels, "because anyone who says they don't exist is full of shit. Do you believe in angels, honey?"

For Christmas Grandma gave me a black coffee mug.

"Go fill it with hot water," she instructed.

As hot water ran into the mug, a ghostly apparition of haphazardly collaged photos appeared, all that same image of Grandma in her twenties.

At midnight we took my girlfriend to the train station. As the train pulled out my mom demanded that I run alongside her window until it was out of sight. The other families stared at me, waiting. "It's romantic!" screamed my mother.

THE HOLE

Today I elbowed my way into a crowd of onlookers. We stood staring down into an enormous gulf, or gorge, I forget which.

I asked the woman next to me what we were looking at. She bit into a potato as though to end its suffering. She looked at me and said a word or maybe two with her mouth full of potato.

I looked at the rest of the gathered crowd, all faces cut down toward the gulch, or gully, I'm not sure which. No one spoke.

There was an air. I thought there was an air of some-thing, of sadness. I thought, certainly, someone has fallen in. Certainly, we are dealing with a tragedy here.

I looked up into the sky.

Someone elbowed his way into the crowd a few feet from me. He looked into the pit.

"What happened?" he asked, looking in my direction.

I gave him a baffled look, kicked a rock into the ravine, or chasm and watched the rock get small and smaller. When I looked up, the other onlookers were looking at me.

WAKEFIELD

My wife. My wife hammers out the things she says. She pounds her way through the words she uses. The things she says to me lie all used up and beaten around the house.

Yesterday, for instance, she tells me, "Poor choice." I was spinning our four-year-old in circles, holding her by her tiny wrists and spinning her around. She laughed and laughed, and I stood her up and she collapsed on the floor and lay there for a minute, eyes crossed.

"That's. Just. Great. Don." my wife said to me.

"Poor. Choice." she said.

This morning I was telling her about this guy at work who has this jittery condition. Some kind of condition that makes him sound like he's laughing while he talks, like everything is so funny to him. She stood there brushing her teeth. I was right in the middle of telling her about this guy, and she spits in the sink and "Jesus. Christ. Don." She says this to me, and gives me a lopsided look and goes downstairs.

Our four-year-old gives me that same lopsided look when she disapproves.

Earlier I sank into my Lay-Z-Boy and when the spring popped I spilled a bowl of macaroni in my lap. My waxen-faced wife looked at me from the couch where she folded laundry.

"You. Have. Got. To. Be. Kidding. Me." a pink towel folded neatly in her lap.

I asked if she would toss me the towel. "Just toss me the towel," I said.

"Not. A. Chance. In. Hell."

I imagined cramming her face in my hot macaroni lap and swiveling it around in there. I stared at her and imagined the couch swallowing her up, sucking her down into the cushions with all the loose change and old hairy Cheetos, nothing left but a basket of warm laundry. Our four-year-old comes trotting in and stands there and gives me that lopsided look.

So there we are: me with my chair and my macaroni, my wife with all those clean towels and our four-year-old with that terrible look on her face.

Charlie Rose was on the TV behind our four-year-old, the volume turned down so the interview was muffled, but I think it was with Cuba Gooding Jr. I asked our four-year-old if she could get out of the way so that I could see the TV better.

"Move, Sweetie," I said.

She ran up the stairs.

"Seriously?" says my gaping wife.

I scooped up what I could of the macaroni and put it back into the bowl.

My wife sighed. My wife let out a sigh, or gave a sigh. She lent a sigh and it was the sweetest thing I had ever heard come from her.

BLUE RIVER ROAD

Behind our house, at the foot of a hill, the woods began and stretched on for miles to a creek where my sister and I sometimes waded. My father positioned a salt lick down near the foot of the hill in order to catch sight of the deer that had been eating his blackberries. Each day he pushed open the sliding glass door with the tips of his fingers and we all quietly stepped out onto the lawn, each with a rifle strapped around a shoulder.

We ate green grapes, passing the bowl around while watching the lick. Over the days, bugs collected on and near the block of salt. Birds and raccoons came and picked at it. My father sometimes threw pebbles and pinecones at them.

We stood through colder nights; sometimes flurries sifted through the trees.

Still we stood in the lawn, passing the bowl and watching the lick.

Snow fell for days until it slowly stopped and a malnourished doe stumbled forward, her long skinny legs sinking deep into the snow. We stopped passing the bowl and watched her pink tongue, like a salmon fillet, scrape at the salt. Her black eye opened wide, watching us watch her lick at the salt.

DEAD SKUNK

(FOR MY SISTER)

We live in a dead skunk town. They stink up the town, the dead skunks. Everywhere you look they are torn apart by cars. We hit the skunks and they are parted up in strands along the roads of our dead skunk town. They are parted up and dead in the dead skunk air and my sister and I breathe it in. We smell it up strong and hold our breath in the backseat of the car. We hold our breath to keep it inside us. We can never get enough of this dead skunk smell. We sit in the backseat on our way to church in this old dead skunk town with our chins tucked into the collars of our pea coats. We sit in our Sunday best with our chins tucked in, weaving wildly through the roads on our way to church in this dead skunk town. Our mother pinches her nostrils in the front seat. Our mother pinches her nostrils and says pew. She says pew and how she hates this dead skunk smell and this dead skunk town. But we, my sister and me, we like it.

RETIREMENT IS A
FLAMINGO POND

When someone retires from the zoo, we toss them into the flamingo pond as a ritual. One of us holds their wrists, and another their ankles. We swing them back and forth; count to three, and in they go, clothes and all, hot pink wings battering a few feet into the air.

The flamingo pond smells severe and sweet like the dark liquid at the bottom of a convenience store dumpster. It is the first thing I smell when I come to work. I can smell it from the parking lot. I have a quick gag reflex and the flamingos make me sick. I can't imagine being tossed in that filthy pond with all that bird excrement and slime. I will never retire for this reason alone. Or maybe I'll be so old when I retire, they won't be able to toss me.

Last year, Diane, one of the docents, retired at the age of seventy-four. When we tossed her in the pond she broke a hip, just from the impact of the water I guess. She sued the director for a hefty sum and they changed the rules to a lower tossing age.

Retirees are always smiling as they swing. A look comes over them that most of us have never seen on their faces before. We always have a good laugh at this, slapping each other on the back. Then we go out to Quigley's for six-dollar pitchers of Bud and baskets of breaded cheese sticks. We laugh and mimic the face of the thrown retiree before and after the tossing.

The conversation usually turns to shop talk, or the time Joe Havershamp, one of the Keepers, lost two fingers to an angry macaw. Joe always laughs along and pretends to pull his hand from the macaw's mouth wiggling his stumps in the air. My wife, one of the docents, loves this charade. She laughs till her eyes water while occasionally gripping Joe's forearm.

She and Joe have been having an affair for months now. I'm almost positive. They are always eyeballing each other when they think I'm not looking. These things happen I suppose. Joe is very charming, in a goofy Tom Selleck kind of way.

I've been having this dream lately, where Joe gets tossed in that putrid flamingo pond. All goes on as it normally does, except he never comes up again.

TV

I have been without TV for three months now and I am so depressed. Without TV I am missing the programs, the many, many programs.

I'm not sure what to do yet without the TV programs. I'm not sure what to make of things, what to make of myself.

I tried reading, but can't stop thinking about the many TV programs.

My wife says it's better, better this way, without TV. I disagree. I need TV, at least to keep updated. I need to feel updated. It is not easy to feel updated without TV.

I am drinking again. Without TV, I turn to drinking, I am not happy about it. Now I am drinking and so depressed.

I went to the bar to drink and watch TV. I watched two programs, two programs I am not a fan of. The one program was about a man who has many partners, many sexual partners, and then he must choose one of them to be his wife forever. That program was ok. The other program was no good, something about two people locked in a house during a storm, no good, that program was no good at all.

It's not the same watching TV programs at the bar. I like to have my feet up on the table, like to eat frozen dinners and watch the many TV programs, like to be able to choose between the many programs. At the bar, the bartender chooses the programs, he never says a word to me, just pours my drinks and watches the TV with his back to me. He watches the TV programs that are his favorites, not mine.

So now it has been three months and I am so depressed and not at all updated. My wife says it's better not to feel updated, says it keeps me fresh, keeps me media free. It keeps you media free, she says to me.

JANUARY

There was movement in the large pile of dead leaves he had set aflame. Black smoke curled into the open air.

"January?"

He said this not as a question, but questioningly.

"January."

His speckled dog, January, might have ventured into the pile and caught fire. Tossing aside a scoop with the rake he saw the source of the rustling. A garden snake lay smoldering in the dirt.

Later that day, he sat quietly at the kitchen table watching out the window. On the table, a plate, on it a paper towel, spotted with grease and folded over three strips of bacon, cold and left over from breakfast.

In the distance a red tailed hawk in the grass ripped strands from a small animal.

"Rabbit," he said.

He looked at the clock, the refrigerator. Stuck on with a magnet was a drawing of a goat his daughter had made long ago. The goat knew something he didn't.

The doggy door flapped and soon January's coarse tongue was repeating itself against his thigh.

A SMALL DEATH

Last year my father gave me a pair of finches for Christmas. They built a nest with the bits of twine I piled in the corner of their cage.

Last night I was playing NFL Football on my PlayStation 3 and I thought the birds were making more noise than usual. I had just scored a touchdown that put my team, the Miami Dolphins, in the lead by seven points when the commotion stopped. I paused the game and walked slowly across the room to the cage.

The finches had curled up together at the bottom of

their empty food dish and died. They were so small in their death, twisted and feathered like a fisherman's flies.

"Goddamnit," I said into the cage.

I had forgotten to feed them. My face burned and my ears tingled. I could hear the Andy Griffith show on the TV. I could smell my father's fried bologna sandwich. I stood there for some time thinking about what the finches were like before they died, fluttering around in the cage.

I emptied out a deck of cards from their box, spilling them across the floor. On the back of the cards were horses galloping through golden fields. I slid the finches into the box and folded the lid shut.

I waited for my father to go to bed before going out back to bury it. The sky swelled over the house. I stood there with the card box and saw the tiny light of an airplane blink away into the dark.

MY HEAD IS A PUNCH BOWL

I was born with a scowl shaped skull, deep in reflection, or in contemplation with everything, with the whole of things. It's hard to say.

My head is a punch bowl. My head feels much too full of punch and not enough moxie. But there it is.

Oh I have interests. I love to see a spray of birds. I am attracted to jars of fancy sea salts.

Mosquitoes, I once read, choose mates who can sing with them in perfect harmony. Two tiny harmonizing hums looking for a warm place to land.

I am not particularly intelligent; I just love certain things to death.

My head is a Brillo box, a kettledrum.

I am not one to form opinions that strike people in the face like a tree branch on a mountain hike. I may not reach emotional maturity until the day I lie shriveled up in bed.

Oh, I have loved and loved. There have been times I thought my chest would burst, leaving hundreds of fish flopping on the beaches. There have been times my eyes swelled from the simple taking in of it all.

My head is a Buick, a bird egg.

Where am I now? A bench, a beach, the sand blooming and dotted with crustaceans. The day is ending, as the mosquitoes have spread out in abundance. I hear their sounds rising and falling away. I sit here with two handfuls of marshmallows. They are repulsive when dissolving in the mouth. Occasionally I throw one into the ocean and watch it float and slip away.

PREGGOS

My high school student asked me the other day... "Say I am pregnant," she said, "and I have sex while I'm pregnant, could my baby get pregnant too?"

"Well," I said to her, "your baby would have to be a girl, but, yes, that could happen, and then, what's worse, if your baby's baby is a girl, then that baby could also become pregnant, and so on."

Her eyes glistened, her lips peeled back. Absolutely horrified.

"Listen, Samantha, I am here for you as a mentor and

a friend, but if you need to talk I would suggest Stephen the school counselor. I've heard he's a good listener and well liked among the students."

She left the room in a sort of bobbing jog, wet cheeked, face contorted, hugging her pink trapper-keeper to her chest.

I put on my jacket and lifted my dangling keys from the pocket.

In the car I waited for the heat to kick on.

In my house I waited for the microwave to beep.

In my bed I waited for the alarm clock to ring.

In the bathroom I waited for my wife to get out of the shower.

In my car I waited for the heat to kick on.

Next day back at school I lecture for an hour on cultural diversity. The children seem vaguely interested, scratching away at their composition notebooks. I show them slides of current events and statistically proven facts. We watch a video about the economy in China; I have them share their thoughts. The children have clearly not been listening. Samantha speaks up. "Is it true people in China cannot have more than two babies? Is it true people in China murder their infant daughters in order to have only boys?"

"These things have some truth to them, yes. Female infanticide, gender-selective abortions. There is, unfortunately a long history of anti-female bias that pervades heavily in patriarchal societies, your examples being the most brutal manifestations of this bias."

When I get home I find my wife in bed with her clone.

They are clinging to each other, I can tell my wife from her clone because we shave the clone's head.

"Jesus, Well this is something," I say, thrown completely off.

"Christ John," says my wife, "I'm sorry, but haven't you ever thought about it?"

No. No I hadn't. I opted out of cloning myself due to the creeps it gives me. Though I suppose a part of me finds two identical wives caught mid-coitus somehow appealing.

Eventually I fall into it and within no time I've impregnated my wife, my wife's clone, the baby in the clone, and the baby's baby.

THE BURIAL

Phyllis is in the bushes. I can see her shifting back and
forth on her haunches, ruffly skirt hiked up over her thighs,
round and white, smooth and thick in their animalness. She
doesn't think I can see her. I know this because she is lipping
and tonguing at a leaf above her head, pretending to be a gi-
raffe or maybe a horse of some kind. Her urine is winding its
way through the mud toward my boots. I step out of its trail. I
see a daddy long-legs scuttling through the mud as if in a panic.
I squat and pinch one of its legs between my fingers and place
it on my nose. It tickles my face as it climbs up into my hair.

Phyllis howls. I'm wondering what time it is and how long it will take to get this over with and go home. I look down at my hands and notice how similar they are to the hands of a chimpanzee's. A woodpecker hacks away at the dead pine above us.

I get back to work. The ground is soft and wet, which is surprising given the frost I had to scrape off my car windows this morning. The shovel sinks in under my muddy work boots. I feel the dead roots crunch and split under my weight. The hole is now about two feet deep and round. Phyllis comes out of the bushes moving the blond strands of hair from her face with a muddy gardening glove. She glances at the cat food bag, which we used to carry her dead cat here to bury. She looks at me and raises her eyebrows and frowns as though about to cry. I stick the shovel in the ground and wipe my hands on my pants.

"Well," I say, "what do you want to do?"

She takes the shovel and starts digging. I light a cigarette, turn and walk, stepping carefully over ferns and flowers.

I can tell I've gone quite a ways when I hear Phyllis howl again in the distance. The woodpecker taps again, far away.

I look up into the trees as I walk and step into what turns out to be a bottomless pit. I am falling endlessly, my coat flapping in the wind. I learn to shift my weight so as to stay mostly upright in a standing position. I cannot light another cigarette and the sound of the wind is deafening. For some time I expect to hit the bottom, maybe water, maybe rock, or at least brush up against the side of the pit, but this will never happen. My panic wanes to sadness and boredom. I am getting thirsty. There is nothing but darkness and wind. I yell but there is no echo, there is almost no sound at all. My eyes burn from the wind so I close them and try to think about better times.

THE RECENT LOCAL
PHENOMENON

Brown bears continue to chew their ways through the telephone poles of our town. They are unrelenting. It is impossible to make a call anymore from a landline. We all have cell phones, but still. Driving through town you see the gnawed up poles toppled over on the roadsides.

The authorities have tried fencing off the poles but the bears chew through the fencing. The authorities tried shooting the bears but the population is out of control.

Paul the butcher who works the deli counter down at the Kroger said the bears sometimes wait in the alley out back for the old fish to be disposed of. Paul poisoned the fish but the bears were resilient, so Paul shot the bears himself and butchered their meat to sell to his customers. One time Paul brought me sixteen pounds of bear meat. Paul dyes all his paper grocery bags black so the blood won't show, but the meat still bled gently through.

Paul has a cleft pallet and drives a Durango.

He is a killer with the ladies.

Last week I woke to find a bear in my living room chewing its way through my coffee table. I put on a robe and called Paul from my cell phone. Paul sounded busy but said he would be right over. The bear curled up on my sofa and fell asleep. I tiptoed to the garage to get a shovel and tiptoed to the bathroom to hide, stepped up on the toilet and squatted there in my robe.

When Paul showed up he was with a lady and they were both loaded. I could hear them from the bathroom cackling and slurring. They came in stumbling around in the dark, knocking over the credenza and spilling my grandmother's vase.

Things got quiet after that.

I stayed in the bathroom till the sun shone through the window.

When I came out I found the three of them, Paul the butcher, his lady, and that big old brown bear curled up asleep on the sofa. I tiptoed to the kitchen to make some coffee and poach some eggs.

The percolator must have woken Paul's lady, because the next thing I heard was a gunshot, and then another. I tiptoed

out to the living room and saw Paul's lady standing there
pointing a smoking pistol, the bear laid out on the carpet,
and Paul on the sofa holding his bloody stomach with one
hand and the keys to his Durango in the other.

MY NOVEL

I did not know where I was. I did not want to know where I was. I lay there in the sun, in the mud. My feet were wet and my back was broken. My nose was broken and my fingers, all of my fingers were broken. I tasted mud in my mouth. My hair was heavy with dried mud, it pulled at my scalp.

There were noises, and animals, the hooves of animals, all around me in the sun, in the mud. I lay with my nose to the sky and the sun. I could not see the animals but I could hear that they were there, trampling and thunking around in the mud, all around me.

I heard the engine of the truck before the animals scattered. I heard them scatter away in the mud. The truck pulled up and stopped. The tire touched the boot on my foot. Touched it just slightly. It was then that someone opened the door and jumped out into the mud, thick in the mud. I felt their hands on my wrists and my head sucking down in the mud as they pulled me out and lifted me into the bed of the truck. My back. My back was broken. And my arms, my arms were also broken.

My novel. My novel was gone. Where was my novel? Christ, where was my novel?

The truck pulled out. My chest hurt and my head bounced in the bed of the truck. I passed out, and then I came to. When I came to, I was lying on a bed of hay being read to softly by my mother.

THE BEAST

Now that the beast has gone, taking his things in a swoop, in a gasp, banging his head on the doorframe on the way out, a grease mark left there, flat and dense, pressed into the wood, I can relax. It's not that I don't love the beast. He used to make me laugh, used to give me pretty things, small, delicate things. Now he grunts and lifts his tail at me. I do not deserve that sort of treatment.

The beast left some of his things here. In his hurry he left a lot of his things in my apartment: his many combs and hair care products, left his sponges and socks. He makes me sick with his stubbornness. I really couldn't care less, but he makes me sick.

Maybe though, I'll just keep his things around in case. Knowing him, he'll come back looking for his things. He'll come back, hair matted up, looking for the rest of his things.

It's not that I don't love him. Actually, I do, to be honest. Actually, I'm not entirely sure what I'll do without him, to be honest, without the beast. He is the only love I've ever known. The beast gives me great pleasure, more pleasure than I've ever known. A great, great deal of pleasure.

SPONSORSHIP

I was goaded into giving up the sponsorship. It would have been nice to know just what I was being sponsored for in the first place. I thought perhaps I was being sponsored for a product I used frequently. Say, Chicken of the Sea, Pabst Blue Ribbon, or Murphy's Oil Soap? But no, that wasn't it.

I telephoned these companies and they seemed to be sponsoring other people.

"What are you talking about, sir?" they asked.

Ok, so maybe it's AIM Toothpaste, Idaho Potato Flakes? Or no, no, it must be the Italian Sausage Prego Pasta Sauce I love so much. I phoned Prego and the woman on the other end thought I was making a joke.

Finally I received a call from the CEO himself. He goaded me, said I had to give it up, said it was too late, no good, said he was the CEO and that I should be glad I still had a pot to piss in. I did still have my pot.

A HANDFUL

Sarah snapped the waistband of her underwear and took another swig of Dr. Pepper. "Don't be cute with me," she said plainly pointing at herself in the full-length mirror. She paused with purpose, posing as in an advertisement. She sang, "Took a midnight-train going an-y-where." She made a face, poking her pink tongue, like a fat wedge of grapefruit into the sharp mouth of the can. A poster of a kitten in a teacup was pinned to the wall. She set the can down and flopped loosely on her bed. She wept with abandon, a pillow clutched over her face, and stopped just as quickly as she had started. She lay in bed staring up at the kitten.

The phone rang. It was Karla.

"Sarah," said Karla.

Sarah said nothing.

"Okay, well, listen, someone mentioned you the other day, they said you always choose the wrong type of guy and I said what? I said, Sarah? Sarah Murphy? and they said yes, yes Sarah always chooses the wrong type of guy, and I said you must be talking about someone else, and they said, oh wait, yeah, I'm talking about someone else, I'm talking about Sarah Mulebach, and I said, who's Sarah Mulebach? And they said, you don't know her."

Sarah breathed dramatically into the phone.

"I have to switch the laundry," she said to Karla, "be right back."

Sarah pranced down the stairs. She loved the feel of the wooly carpet between her toes. She turned the corner and slipped into the kitchen where her mother was chopping onions. A package of gummy bears lay mangled on the counter. Sarah snatched a handful, pressed them in her mouth, winked at her mother, turned the corner, and pranced down the wooden steps to the basement.

Pulling the clothes from the dryer, she found the sleeves of shirts had become twisted and tied around towels and pant legs. It reminded her of that awful clown on her sixth birthday, pulling an endless string of colored paper from his mouth.

She set the dial on the dryer, pressed the button, leapt up the stairs, snatched another handful, pressed them into her mouth, winked, flew up the second flight and flopped on the bed.

Karla was singing incoherently into the phone.

"Okay," muffed Sarah, mouth still full of bears.

"Oh good," said Karla, "So, about that little problem you're having, I talked to my brother, and he said he knows how to get rid of it."

Sarah sat up and spat the chewed ball of gummy bears into her free hand. It was dazzling to look at, glistening like a cheap plastic brooch.

ROAD TRIP

I blew out a tire. Felt the flump flump of it beneath me. I imagined the shredded rubber curling on the highway. I pulled over and got out. There were no other cars around. The fall leaves swayed and brushed into each other. A dead possum lay opened up in the grass, just bone and fur. I leaned over to get a closer look. Its teeth were perfect looking. 'I wish my teeth were that perfect,' I thought.

I went into my hatchback, pulled out a sleeveless shirt and put it on. I got out the spare and thought of sparing. I thought, 'a spare,' something kept in case another something of the same type is lost, or broken. I thought, 'spare me.' If my car could think, it would probably think, 'spare me.'

I walked to the passenger side and saw that my girlfriend was still asleep. Probably exhausted from all the crying. I knocked lightly on the glass and she opened her eyes without moving, then closed them.

I pulled the jack open, walked back and slid it under the car.

There are so many scenarios that have, that could have taken place, while jacking up one's car, while changing one's tire.

My girlfriend yelled my name, her voice muffled from the inside. I stood and walked to her door. She rolled down the window without opening her eyes, her face surrounded by a huge rabbit fur hood.

"What have you done?" she asked.

I looked away and down the road.

I reached into the backseat and found the bag of carrots. Walked straight into the woods and peed on a tree, carrot protruding from my mouth.

SALLY

Sally climbed the stairs three at a time as she did every morning after breakfast. This may have been unwise, as she was growing old. Regardless of the danger, she found it exhilarating and would have it no other way. Today however, she had to steady herself on the windowsill at the top of the staircase.

She saw in the yard below, a man in all denim, digging a hole. She tried to focus on him, she told herself this would help, but couldn't seem to keep her vision from spinning. Above the man the leaves of the maple were wonderfully orange and yellow, and above them the sky glowered down at her. The dark sky scared her a little, she thought it very odd indeed and tightened her grip on the sill, her nails sinking into the soft wood.

When she looked back down to the yard, she saw that the man had finished digging, and had in fact climbed down into the hole and disappeared. Her head swam. She pressed her cheek against the cold glass and watched for the man to reemerge. The wind made the maple shudder. She thought it strange how silent the tossing tree was from this side of the window. It should make a sound, she thought, but it didn't.

I NO LONGER NEED HIM

I am a versatile woman with a penchant for expensive
white wine and fried chicken dinners. My husband tends to
display his doctoral degree out from under the gray bristles
on his upper lip to anyone within ear-shot, even when, as
of now, he has been evicted from his place of employment,
i.e., laid off. Although my husband, in his prime, kept his
banana-cream waves shoulder-length, looking much like
the actor Michael Douglas in the roaring 1984 film *Romanc-
ing the Stone*, these follicles have experienced a significant
recession. Now he holds beneath his slumping chest the

protrusion of belly commonly found on men his width in years.

I no longer need him the way that I once thought I should wrench the muscles to feel that thing that they call need. It's true that on occasion an old mounting motivation moves my husband to escort me to the bedroom where we integrate, as if to become again what we once were. These moments are spent, not locked in an ear to ear eschewal, as most ideas of failing couplets would have it, but staring directly into the eyes of one another, his brown, mine green, without so much as a smidge of recognition.

Some time ago we bore a child after one of these moments. Rather it was I who bore it, he simply watched dog-eyed from the sidelines.

Throughout the entire twelve hours of labor I could not get a specific memory, or was it a dream, out from under my head. I stood in a snowy ditch decked out in a camouflage jump suit taking dead aim down the sites at a ten-point buck. The occasional shuddering of its hide and the wet flaring of its deep black nostrils had me utterly mesmerized.

I contracted and pushed and felt the thing wriggling in there, trying to get out.

FROZEN DINNER

I went to the store to buy a frozen dinner. I kept my head down through the aisles. I found the frozen food aisle, a long stretch of frosty glass doors. I found the frozen dinners, stacks of them behind the frosty doors. I saw myself in the glass, staring back. I saw my reflection in the glass separating me from the frozen dinners. I could see my eyes on the cover of a Salisbury steak frozen dinner. I changed the focus of my eyes, to focus on the reflection of my eyes, to the frozen Salisbury steak dinner, and then back to focus on the reflection of my eyes. I was so tired from the night before.

I opened the frosty door and was hit by frosty air and closed the door without getting the frozen dinner. Now the door was frosty and foggy and I could not see the frozen dinners. I looked down the aisle and saw a woman holding a kid by the arm, holding him up so that his feet barely touched the ground. The kid was crying and the woman was angry, holding the kid by the arm. I looked down the other way and saw a man with a price gun, tagging the frozen foods. The man was on his knees. I looked back to the frozen dinners and again saw my reflection staring back at me in the foggy door.

This time I made a sort of face at myself; I made a sort of 'what are you looking at?' face with my eyebrows up and my mouth a little open. I pulled my sleeves down over my hands. I pinched the closest frozen dinner and left the frozen food aisle. I paid for the frozen dinner and left the store.

When I got to my car I looked in the bag and saw I'd bought the fried chicken frozen dinner. The fried chicken frozen dinner comes with a compartment of mashed potatoes, a compartment of peas and carrot cubes, a compartment of fried chicken, two wings and a thigh, and a compartment of cherry rhubarb.

THE PUNISHMENT

We had to kill Molly. It was a sunrise execution. The gnats had just started to pop up from the wet gray grass, and the cicadas were quieting down. We walked her in chains across the grounds and into a meadow where a pit had been dug the night before. I walked alongside, holding her by the ear, feeling the heat it gave off. Her eyes said nothing to me. They stared without recognition, without a hint of feeling.

Molly's weaving had been bad lately. I used to watch her slowly sway her head. I used to beg her to stop. These habits are unhealthy, I would tell her. I used to talk to her for hours in the old barn, about my childhood mostly, and she would listen and sway her head.

We weren't expecting rain, but right as we neared the pit it came and came steady. She slumped down to her knees in the pit, rain beating down on her dark body, down on myself and the rest of the crew, who looked like dark cut outs against the pale sky. I slipped into the pit with her and leaned heavily against her body. I felt the wet roughness of her skin against my face.

Dr. Havershamp slipped down into the mud with us and instructed me to pull her ear back. He injected thirteen grains of strychnine behind her ear with a large needle. She crumpled over on her side, trembling.

There was a time when the children of this town loved Molly. They would come running to her, cheering and pleading to climb on her back.

Now I pressed myself against her until I felt her giant heart stop beating.

THERE IS A HOUSE THERE

There is a house there. There are strangers in my house there? It is full of strangers. I am there. I live there. It is my house (well I'm renting). In the back of the house is a creek but there are no rocks in it.

(Sudden dialogue)

"There are no rocks in the creek?"

"Nope."

There is a rumbling upstairs. Mice or raccoons I think, their mouths full of rocks. There are traps set but they are in the basement. The traps are set with grape jelly and miniature springs. The springs pop and snap the wires shut on the necks of mice when they come to lick at the clusters of jelly.

There are no traps for the raccoons.

There is no way to deter them.

There aren't any ways to.

The house is large enough for them to be there without ever seeing me there, or I them there.

I like to think that the house has a grand ballroom. The room's ceiling is lit with crystal chandeliers. There are white-gowned tables and a paisley patterned wallpaper the color of butter.

But it doesn't, the house I mean, have a ballroom in it.

We dispose of the mice bodies...mouse bodies...the small bodies, are disposed of, traps and all, by bucket, to the creek, for the fox to have their way with.

I say *we* dispose, well, that's due to there are strangers there, but no, they are not "strangers." I have known them my entire life.

(Narrator exits, pursued by a bear)

WHEN I'M FEELING UP TO IT

My wife is a cistern for whatever comes her way. This morning I saw her painfully trying to shove her tongue into the small sharp mouth of a yogurt cup. I watched from the crack where the bedroom door folds into the wall. I could see her head moving back and forth to extend her tongue further into the cup, to rotate it, scooping the yogurt remains.

I am a pathetically breakable husband, unworthy and unwilling to get any better. I lost any idea of getting any better a long time ago.

My wife used to have poodley long hair, used to wear pink windbreaker outfits and interesting footgear. Now she is made up and perfumy, now she scowls and glares and stomps away from me to her rocking chair on the porch.

I realize I am just getting by.

When I'm feeling up to it, I usher her fitfully to the bedroom where we form a temporary pile with one another. The top of us, seen from above, or possibly from the side, would look like a shifting plummeting baby hippopotamus. Would look about to burst or hurt, or have a moment, taking itself aback, as to take or be taken, taken away, taken with, taken away with, taken to or from. As she took me, I was taken by her. She shook me and I was...well you get the idea.

And when it was over I took to sitting near the back door, took to concentrating on the grass through which in time I intended to push the mower. Intended to scrap what was trying too hard, living too well, if only to keep up appearances.

BRASS TACKS

I woke up freezing in the cab of my pickup truck. I could tell by the light loom of blue in the sky it was hardly dawn. I sat up and saw that I was in the desert, and certainly not near any road. The desert was flat and then no longer flat toward the horizon. I put my fingers in my mouth and pulled out a tooth. I studied the texture of the tooth between my fingers and picked at its cracks. I looked up and the new light had turned everything pale.

I started the truck. It took three tries but it started. I drove carefully through, or over, the desert, over patches of crabgrass and mounds of rock-sand. I stuck my tongue in the hole where my tooth once was and drove easily through the desert until I came upon the Desert Wildlife Preserve. I put the tooth in a pill bottle after spilling the pills on the floor of the cab. I was drowsy.

I purchased a ticket to the Preserve. It was an outdoor Preserve and so I followed a long path through what seemed to be the same desert I had just come in out of. I passed a large family of Javelinas. In their hot black eyes I saw a darkness that moved me to whimper and step backward and away.

Further up the path I saw a small group of people gathering in the brush so I rushed to join them. I saw through the sleeves of the group, through their rubbing shoulders and shifting legs, a woman in a brown uniform, holding on her uplifted arm a beautiful bird of prey. She lifted her arm and the bird thinned out across the horizon and perched on a distant saguaro where a long strand of red meat had been hung for it.

A cell phone rang in the crowd. The man in front of me answered without saying hello. He wore a bright red cardigan.

"I'm also…I'm writing a book of jokes too," he said after a moment. It was very quiet in the Preserve.

"Letterman is a dick, but it's not like anyone's going to hold that against him."

The wind picked up a little and tossed the crowd's hair just a bit and all at once. His voice became whispery, mean and quick. I leaned forward.

"Well Lorraine, how do *you* relax in the summer? Huh? What kinds of things do *you* do?"

No one else seemed to notice. Or maybe they were just waiting there like me. Waiting for the bird to come back. Waiting for Lorraine to respond.

"Tom Cruise," he whispered angrily.

"Tom Cruise, Tom *Cruise*."

People were staring. The man shouldered me on his way out of the crowd.

"Brass tacks *Lorraine*," I heard him say as he walked away, "I will eat the Jesus *Christ* out of anything you put in front of me and you know it."

I watched him weave his way around the long desert path until he was just a small speck of red in the sand.

I AM A NATURAL WONDER

I grew a mustache way too early and happily combed its delicate length every morning before school. The other children looked on in admiration, their lunch trays heavy with stiff Salisbury steaks and the bloated deliciousness of Hostess cherry fruit pies.

Samantha never seemed to notice. It was Samantha I wished to impress.

I once cricked my neck admiring her. Well worth it, well worth it! Had to stay home for a day. My nose bled as usual so I fed it to the cat, which lapped the blood up greedily from my lips. In the shower I cried, but from elation you understand! For breakfast I microwaved a croissant and jacked it open with a finger until the hole was big enough to wiggle my tongue into.

My mother spent the afternoon guzzling pork-slap and slathering mayo on warm white bread. My father drove through town looking desperately for lumber. I sat swaddled in a blue sheet watching *The Price is Right*, twisting the corners of my mustache, and thinking of Samantha.

After a while the crick wore off and I walked to the Piggly Wiggly to troll the aisles for a snack.

Outside, a black-fisted giant poked a long finger into the open mouth of a gumball machine. Something was lodged in the way. His daughter straddled a stationary galloping horse with fire painted in its eyes.

Inside I bought a jar of pearl onions from a cashier who stared directly down into the trellis of my mustache.

At home my big brother smoked Old Golds wearing his thick-skinned deer gloves. He was always reading some book called *Desert Tooth*. His mustache was twice as long as mine, but he was twice as old. He had a date with a Chinese girl. I asked him again what he was reading and he reached deep into his mouth with his fingers and threw gum at me.

The phone rang out and I stumbled into the kitchen. It was Samantha. Could I go swimming in Old Blue with balloons in our underwear to keep us afloat?

Certainly, I said.

REDOLENT SON

(FOR MY MOTHER)

.

One day I was asleep on my mother's couch. One day I was twenty-seven years old and asleep on her couch and I woke up and she's standing there, standing there over me and she says to me, you smell the same, you smell the same she says to me, I remember the day you came out of me you smelled that way, I smell you now and you smell the same to me. I'll never forget that smell, she said.

I smelled myself and thought of death. I thought, I smell like something left to stink in the sun, like a damp ditch off a busy highway. I smell like a man who hasn't quite grown up, who emits smells that others might find repulsive.

Yes, there was something comforting in it, something some might wish to curl up next to, or nuzzle a nose into, or take home in a T-shirt and stuff under a pillow. But a distinct stench still lived somewhere in there, something of shoe rot and basement bedroom, something of cake icing and reptile cage.

My mother, whose smell I can't recall at all, looked down at me with a very young face, much younger than her usual face. I'll never, ever, forget that smell, she said.

INTO THE WOODS

Caught a crawdad in the creek and scrambled through the woods to show my mother, who was washing dishes. I could not breathe when I found her there and so lifted the crawdad well above my head for her to see. She smiled and brought down a bowl to put it in.

I took it to the bathroom, filled up the sink with water and carefully lifted the crawdad in. Closed and locked the door. Stood on the toilet and opened the mirror-cabinet. Quickly ate a cough drop and spat cherry-red into the crawdad's sink water. I drained the sink and watched the crawdad try to scuttle up the side, pinching with its claws. I sat on the toilet, put my chin on the cold sink, and watched the crawdad, and the crawdad, I thought, watched me.

The sky was nearly too dark to see when I came back outside with the crawdad in the bowl. I said the pledge of allegiance to the flag and danced around in circles, holding the bowl to the sky. Found my yellow wiffle ball bat buried halfway in the dirt. Put the bowl on the ground and picked up the bat and the crawdad by its tail, tossed it straight up into the sky and hit it deep into the woods. It arched over the trees and into the dark woods; I did not hear it land.

A CONFLUENCE OF
OCCURRENCES

My father used to leave exotic body parts in the freezer. He always had a good chuckle when one of us jumped at the sight. One time I went in for a grape Otter-pop and there was this head of a zebra staring back at me. Its eyes bulged out cartoony and its lips peeled back over these huge yellow teeth. My sister found hippo parts in the pantry and a box of wildebeest horns in the garage. My father said this was all due to a lack of refrigeration space at the zoo, and that he needed to study the specimens.

One day my mother discovered the furry arm of a

gibbon wrapped in newsprint. She slammed the gibbon's arm on the kitchen table and said, "Enough."

There was a loud bang from next door. My father went to check it out and came back as pale as skim milk. Our neighbor, Mr. Havershamp, had shot himself. My mother put her hand to her mouth.

My first thought was of Mr. Havershamp's children, Pete and Muffin. I had had little interaction with the Havershamps, ever since I found little Muffin in the garage making sculptures out of dog feces.

My memories of Mr. Havershamp were vague and spaced out over many years. I had often seen him passing from one room to another. I had seen him looking dejected, now that I think of it, mowing his lawn.

Mr. Havershamp had shot himself while his wife slept in the bed next to him. This was a cruel decision, I thought. My father changed into his coveralls and went over to clean up the mess, scrubbing brains from the ceiling and whatnot, I imagine. He was used to unforgettable scenes.

I never did see Pete again. Muffin now waits tables at the local Lizard's Thicket. I do love their warm buttery biscuits, but I can never bring myself to dine there.

ALTERED BEAST

We used to throw abandoned TV sets over the railing and watch them explode on the railroad tracks below. Once there was half a bowling ball with blue inner rings like a bitten Everlasting Gobstopper, and a mini-fridge filled with Taco Bell hot sauce packets. We threw those over as well.

This bridge was in the woods on a dead end dirt road. A few miles away, junky apartment buildings stood dejected in a clearing. The apartment grounds had a rusty green swing set and a busted teeter-totter but there never were any kids playing. The families in these apartments would haul their difficult trash to the end of this road and leave it in a heap on the bridge.

Throwing this trash over gave it one last purpose. Gave each object its own ending.

One time, Junior, drunk on peppermint schnapps, threw his BMX over the railing. His gesture was more exciting than the slightly twisted result. He had to walk home and lie to his parents that the bike was stolen.

My father remarried a woman with more money than we had, so we moved out of our small rental in Red Bridge to a meringue colored split-level in a neighborhood named Bridlespur. I made friends fairly quickly, and we were never apart.

Our typical afternoons were spent either at the bridge throwing trash or at the bowling alley where we played long games of *Double Dragon* and *Altered Beast*. We'd go out back to smoke the Virginia Slims Teddy took off his mother and there Crazy Dave would be in his sea-green hospital scrubs, stepping quietly back and forth as if in a panic.

Other times we'd see Crazy Dave wearing the same hospital scrubs and pacing the flowered median that split Red Bridge road in two. From a distance we would wave at him and laugh, each of us too afraid to taunt further than that.

I secretly believed I'd end up just like him, pacing the length of the road I grew up on, wearing a stained bathrobe and mumbling broken ideas to myself. This possibility scared me more than anything else. My waves at Crazy Dave became sincere and saddened. He never did wave back.

ANOTHER DAY AT THE A&P

I have stalked all the vegetables, carefully smelling each one, careful to pull the bad ones and put them in a bin, bruised apples and bell peppers spotted with white hairy mold. I have piled the fruits carefully, sometimes eating a grape, or shaking a coconut. But there is an air of coldness in here today, under all these fluorescent lights. Not a soul has come in to buy any-thing—the lights are on, the doors are open, but there is no one here. The brown paper sacks are stacked high and bound with twine. The aisles are mopped and all the canned goods have been pulled forward, labels turned outward.

Still there is no one here but me. I have collected every cart from the parking lot, pushing them in a long rickety line through the automatic doors. I have wiped down every freezer door and thrown out every day-old donut. I have cleaned and waxed the sushi counter and rotated every milk carton. I walk slowly through the store, careful to turn my head. Nothing. I have broken down all the boxes. I have priced all the frozen foods. I have counted and recounted all the money in the tills. I'll have to lock up and go home soon. I have been alone all day in my green apron and my orthopedic shoes.

MY FRIEND'S FATHER

My friend's father worked difficult nights in a dilapidated donut factory. The factory was in the Bottoms. My friend and his father lived in a house with no windows down by the Bottoms. Long lengths of wood-like paneling covered every wall. My friend's father played the classic rock station at all hours. My friend and I took our Tonka trucks into the empty closets and played with them in there. We wanted to get away from the classic rock and so we went into the closets where it was muffled by the wood paneling and the peach colored carpet. My friend's father had a mustache and drank beer from a tall can. Their house was always so dark and so empty. They had no furniture in their house, no windows and no furniture, only carpeting and paneling and closets and beer.

One night I was staying over at my friend's house and his father had to work so he took us along. Only one seatbelt worked in the backseat of my friend's father's car so he buckled us together. We drove through the Bottoms listening to the classic rock station and looking out the window. The streets in the Bottoms were brick, so we drove slowly over them, past the old brick buildings. It was so dark and so cold in the Bottoms at night but the sky for some reason was mud orange and low slung over us.

My friend's father was made to deliver donuts in a bearclaw truck to convenience stores around town. My friend and I sat on boxes in the back of the bearclaw truck eating pastries and pies. Our faces and fingers were sticky with them.

We ate fritters and crullers and jellies and glazed, frosted and crumb and crème filled, powdered and even plain. We were sick with them.

It was early morning by the time we got back to the factory. The sky had mulled into a pale gray and the birds had taken to it. My friend's father went to collect his pay and my friend and I weighed ourselves on a giant scale meant for the bearclaw truck. The numbers came up big and red on a screen above the garage door. First I weighed myself and then my friend weighed himself, and then we stood on it together. Even together we weighed almost nothing at all.

ACKNOWLEDGMENTS

Thanks to the journals that published stories from this collection:

"The Observable Characteristics of Organisms" first appeared in *American Short Fiction* where it won first place for the 2012 American Short(er) Fiction Prize. "My Friend's Father" in *notnostrums*. "The Storm" and "The Beast" in *Fast Forward Press*; "CHiPS" and "Into the Woods" in *NOÖ Weekly*; "Tell me with whom you walk and I will tell you who you are" and "The Burial" in *Route Nine;* and "Urgebirge" in *Fountain Studios' Chrome.*

Thanks to Noy Holland for her remarkable powers. Without Noy this wouldn't exist. Thanks to Aretha Aoki for her sweet patience and hard work helping me put this together. Thanks to my extraordinary friends and family, all of you. Thanks to Jordan Stempleman and his invaluable support, and to his family Marlee, Bella, and Townes for being my family as well. Thanks to Phyllis Moore for her astounding encouragement and guidance. Thanks to Kim Hennessy, Nick Partridge, and Hutch Partridge for their friendship and providing a quiet space to edit. Thanks to the board members at FC2, and to Dan Waterman and the University of Alabama Press.